READING CHAMPION

Abdul's Lazy Sons

by Katie Dale and Shahab Shamshirsaz

W
FRANKLIN WATTS
LONDON • SYDNEY

There was once a farmer called Abdul.

He had three sons: Hakim, Jamal and Malik.

All year long, Abdul worked hard on the farm.

But his lazy sons did nothing to help him.

Hakim

Jamal

Malik

3

In the spring, Abdul ploughed the fields.

"Will you help me, Hakim?" he asked.

Hakim was gazing at himself in the mirror.

"How handsome I look," he thought.

"If I help plough the fields, I'll get very dirty."

"Sorry, Father, I can't help you!" he said.

In the hot summer, Abdul watered

the dry fields.

"Jamal, will you help me?" he asked.

Jamal was lazing in the shade.

"I'm so comfortable and cool," Jamal thought.

"If I help water the fields, I'll get hot and sweaty.

I won't go."

He closed his eyes and pretended to be asleep.

In the autumn, Abdul harvested the crops.

"Will you come and help me, Malik?" he asked.

Malik was just about to eat his dinner.

"If I help harvest the crops, my food
will get cold," Malik thought.

"Not now, Father!" he called.

Abdul's sons wouldn't help him sell the crops at market either ...

... but they wanted the money he earned.

"My sons are so vain and greedy and lazy,"

thought poor Abdul.

He decided to teach them a lesson.

The next day, Abdul pretended to be ill in bed.

"Now they'll have to run the farm

by themselves!" he thought.

But a few days later, Abdul overheard his sons talking. They were very worried.

"Father's too ill to work, and we're running out of food," Malik said. "What should we do?"

"There's only one thing we can do," said Hakim. "We'll have to sell the farm."

Jamal and Malik agreed.

Poor Abdul couldn't believe his ears.

His plan hadn't worked and now his sons

were going to sell his farm. This was a disaster!

Then Abdul had a very clever idea.

"You can't sell the farm! There's gold hidden

in the fields!" he called out to his sons.

"Gold?" the brothers cried. "We'll be rich!"

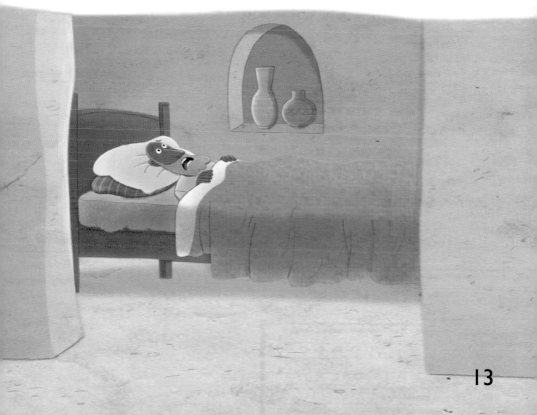

Abdul had never seen his sons move so fast.

They hurried outside to the fields.

They began to dig. At first, digging was

hard work. But after a while they began

to enjoy it.

Hakim's muscles grew big and strong.

Malik enjoyed digging up vegetables

for his dinner. Jamal wasn't worried when

he got hot and sweaty.

They spent weeks digging every inch
of the fields. But they didn't find any gold.
"We'll have to sell the farm after all,"
sighed Malik.

"No! Wait one more year," Abdul said.

"I'm feeling better now, so I'll help you search.

We'll find the gold, I'm sure. If we don't,

you can sell the farm then."

The brothers agreed. Every day, they helped dig the fields and collect water for the crops. Abdul looked at the fields. He was amazed when he saw how hard his sons had worked.

The soil was soft, with no weeds or rocks.

There was enough water for things to grow.

The crops grew bigger and better than ever.

When Abdul went to market to sell the crops, his sons came too. They got a lot of money. "My sons, here is the gold I promised you," Abdul smiled. "You've earned it."

The brothers laughed happily.

"The gold **was** hidden in the fields!"

said Jamal. "But not in the way we thought!"

The brothers hugged their clever father,

and they were never lazy again.

Story order

Look at these 5 pictures and captions.
Put the pictures in the right order
to retell the story.

1

Abdul pretended to be ill.

2

Abdul and his sons went to market.

3

Abdul told them there was hidden gold.

4

Abdul's sons never helped him.

5

The sons worked hard in the fields.

Independent Reading

This series is designed to provide an opportunity for your child to read on their own. These notes are written for you to help your child choose a book and to read it independently.

In school, your child's teacher will often be using reading books which have been banded to support the process of learning to read. Use the book band colour your child is reading in school to help you make a good choice. *Abdul's Lazy Sons* is a good choice for children reading at Gold Band in their classroom to read independently.

The aim of independent reading is to read this book with ease, so that your child enjoys the story and relates it to their own experiences.

About the book

Abdul's sons are lazy, greedy and vain. They do nothing to help their father on the farm. Abdul pretends to be ill to force them to start working, but it nearly ends in them selling his farm. Then he cleverly plays a trick on them to show the value of hard work.

Before reading

Help your child to learn how to make good choices by asking: "Why did you choose this book? Why do you think you will enjoy it?" Look at the cover together and ask: "What do you think the story will be about?" Ask your child to think of what they already know about being lazy. Then ask your child to read the title aloud. Ask: "Do you think Abdul is happy that his sons are lazy?" Remind your child that they can sound out the letters to make a word if they get stuck.

Decide together whether your child will read the story independently or read it aloud to you.

During reading

Remind your child of what they know and what they can do independently. If reading aloud, support your child if they hesitate or ask for help by telling the word. If reading to themselves, remind your child that they can come and ask for your help if stuck.

After reading

Support comprehension by asking your child to tell you about the story. Use the story order puzzle to encourage your child to retell the story in the right sequence, in their own words. The correct sequence can be found on the next page.

Help your child think about the messages in the book that go beyond the story and ask: "Why do you think Abdul played this trick on his sons? Do you think they would have learned the same lesson if he had just told them to help him?"

Give your child a chance to respond to the story: "Have you ever been unhelpful when you have been asked for help? Have you ever helped someone who has asked for help? Which felt better?"

Extending learning

Help your child predict other possible outcomes of the story by asking: "If the sons had not helped Abdul on the farm, what do you think might have happened? Do you think they would have kept on being lazy? Would they have to start working anyway?"

In the classroom, your child's teacher may be teaching contractions. There are many examples in this book that you could look at together, including *I'll* (I will), *can't* (cannot), *I'm* (I am), *won't* (will not), *wouldn't* (would not), *they'll* (they will), *we're* (we are), *there's* (there is), *we've* (we have). Find these together and point out how the apostrophes are used in place of the omitted letters.

Franklin Watts
First published in Great Britain in 2018
by The Watts Publishing Group

Series Editors: Jackie Hamley and Melanie Palmer
Series Advisors: Dr Sue Bodman and Glen Franklin
Series Designer: Peter Scoulding

A CIP catalogue record for this book is
available from the British Library.

ISBN 978 1 4451 6239 3 (hbk)
ISBN 978 1 4451 6241 6 (pbk)
ISBN 978 1 4451 6240 9 (library ebook)

Printed in China

Franklin Watts
An imprint of
Hachette Children's Group
Part of The Watts Publishing Group
Carmelite House
50 Victoria Embankment
London EC4Y 0DZ

An Hachette UK Company
www.hachette.co.uk

www.franklinwatts.co.uk

Answer to Story order: 4, 1, 3, 5, 2